Woof
A Love Story

By Sarah Weeks

Illustrated by

Holly Berry

Laura Geringer Books
An Imprint of HarperCollins Publishers

Woof: A Love Story
Text copyright © 2009 by Sarah Weeks
Illustrations copyright © 2009 by Holly Berry

Manufactured in China.

Library of Congress Cataloging-in-Publication Data
Weeks, Sarah.
    Woof: a love story / by Sarah Weeks ; illustrated by Holly Berry. —1st ed.
        p. cm.
    Summary: Despite a language barrier, a dog and cat fall in love with the help of a buried
trombone.
    ISBN 978-0-06-025007-2 (trade bdg.) — ISBN 978-0-06-025008-9 (lib. bdg.)
    [1. Dogs—Fiction. 2. Cats—Fiction. 3. Communication—Fiction. 4. Love—
Fiction. 5. Stories in rhyme.] I. Berry, Holly, ill. II. Title.
PZ8.3.W4215Br 2009   2006022295
[E]—dc22   CIP
                                                            AC

10   11   12   13   SCP   10   9   8   7   6   5
❖
First Edition

For Brian Selznick.
Meow, S.W.

To my beloved Chris
—H.B.

A dog is a dog
and a cat is a cat,
And most of the time
it's as simple as that.

Most of the time
    what a dog has in mind
Is doing "dog" things
    with the rest of his kind:

Running and panting,

sniffing and growling,

Rolling in things, digging and howling.

But this story begins on a fine spring day
With a dog who got up in the usual way.
He yawned and he stretched,
Then he sniffed at the air

And found something very *un*usual there.

That's when she saw him, this humongous hound,
Taking the steps in a single bound.

And under her fur she turned terribly pale.

She was white from her tail to the tip of her nose,
Which was tiny and pink as a cake-frosting rose.
His heart began thumping so hard in his chest,
He thought lying down for a while might be best.

He lay in the grass and stared up at the cat.
She glared down at him from the tree where she sat.
After a bit, he lifted his head—
Opened his mouth—
and here's what he said:

I love
you!

He meant to say that, there is no doubt,

But

woof
woof woof
woof

was what really came out.

She climbed up instead.

He said every flowery wallpaper word,
But woof, woof, woof, woof, woof, woof, woof's
what she heard.
He finally gave up. He was blue as the sea.

I quit,

he announced.
"You don't understand me."

He turned and he left, with his ears hanging low.
She wondered, "Why has he decided to go?"
Instead of attacking, he left her behind,
And she thought,

Hmm, this dog must
be one of a kind.

When a dog's low and his troubles seem big,
One thing that may help cheer him up is to dig.
He'll dig and he'll dig 'til his spirits are lifted,
And things can turn up in the dirt that he's sifted.
Sometimes a coin or a shoe or a stone,
But this doggie dug up—a shiny brass bone.

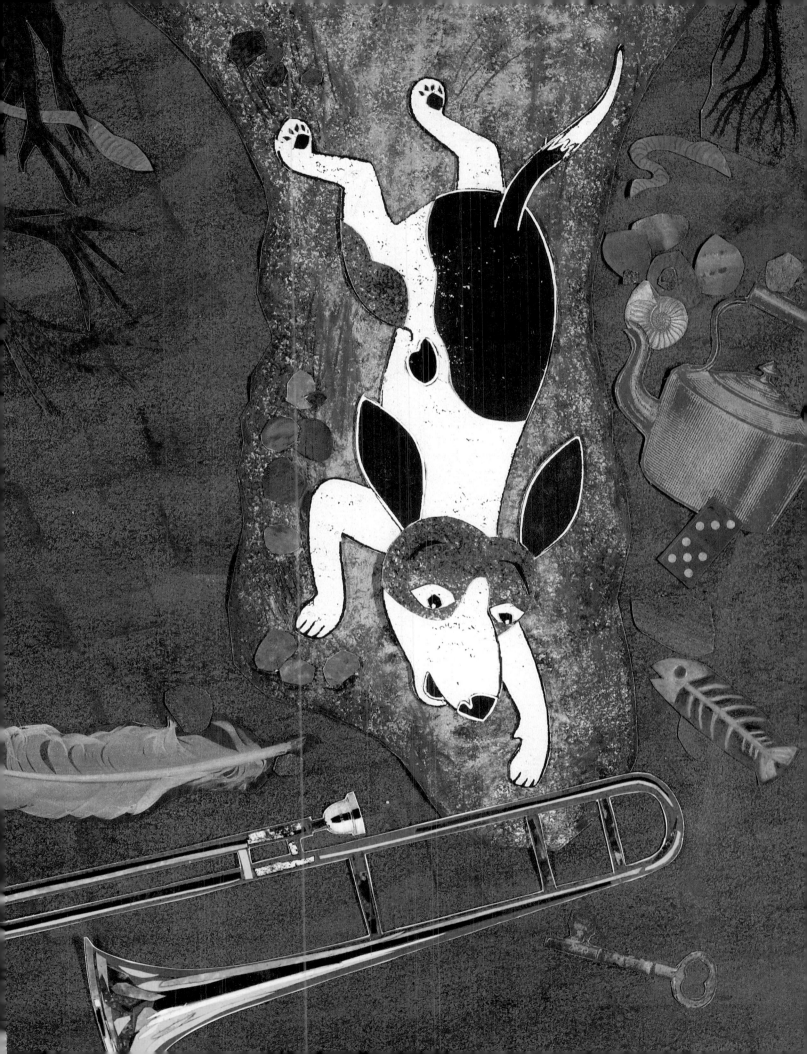

He pulled this enormous gold thing from the ground,
And he blew in the end of it—my! What a sound.
At first he just splatted and blatted about,

But then something different began to pour out.

He had all these powerful feelings inside,
So strong and so deep they could not be denied.
He blew in the stuff he was thinking about,
And all of a sudden this MUSIC came out.

The minute she heard the sweet music he made,
She understood just what he felt when he played.

He played the brass bone while she sat on the limb,
And when he had finished, she climbed down to him.
He looked in her eyes and he laid down the bone,
And took her tiny white paw in his own.
At first she was shy, then she lifted her head,
Opened her mouth, and quietly said,

In truth what she said was, *Meow.*
But he understood what she meant anyhow.